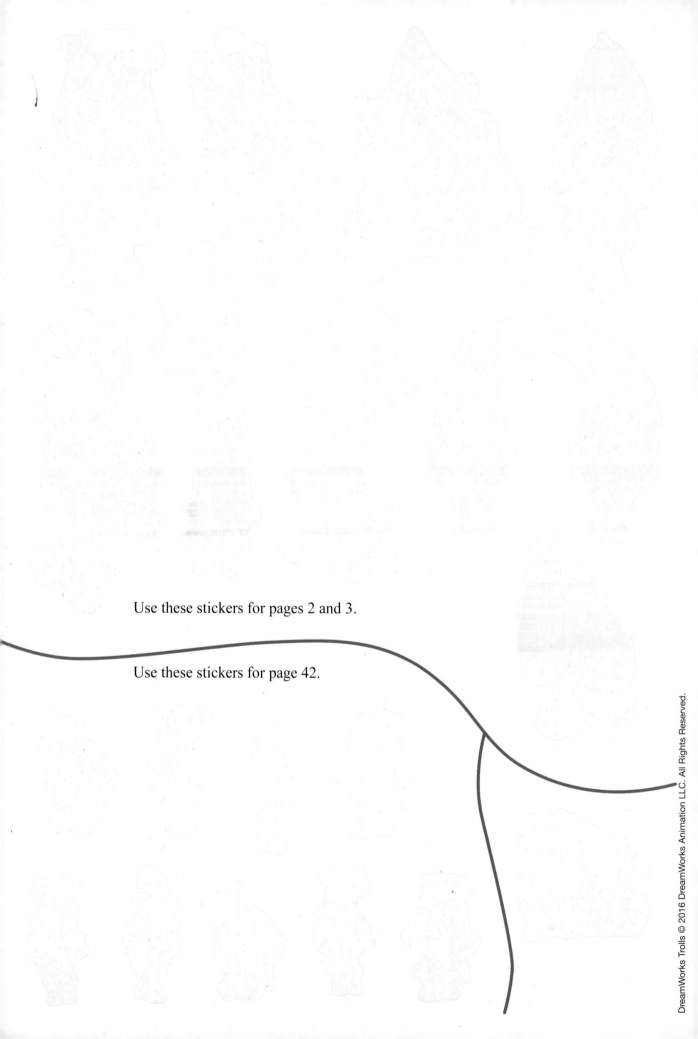

Use these stickers for pages 2 and 3.

Use these stickers for page 42.

HUGFEST

PASS THE GLITTER!

Have a Hair-ific Day!

SHOW YOUR TRUE COLORS

HUG

HUGFEST

BIGGEST LOUDEST CRAZIEST PARTY EVER!

HUGS all Around

PUT YOUR HAIR in the AIR

Have a Hair-ific Day!

dance hug sing

PASS THE GLITTER!

ROCK N TROLL

great vibes!

PARTY!

LET'S DANCE!!!

HUG

LOVE IS IN the HAIR

SHOW YOUR TRUE COLORS

Spread the Hugs

HUGS all Around

BIGGEST LOUDEST CRAZIEST PARTY EVER!

LOVE IS IN the HAIR

Wanna hug?

Good Friends

From yours TROLLY

Have a Glitter Day!

BE UNIQUE

DOUBLE the hugs

LOVE IS IN the HAIR

Troll·la·la!

QUEEN POPPY

QUEEN POPPY

U could use a HUG

U could use a HUG

DON'T smug Give a hug!

HUG YOUR HEART OUT

SMILE HUG REPEAT

Queen of HUGS!

HAVE a glitter day!

Trolls

Love is in the Hair!

By Rachel Chlebowski

A GOLDEN BOOK • NEW YORK

DreamWorks Trolls © 2016 DreamWorks Animation LLC. All Rights Reserved. Published in the United States by Golden Books, an imprint of Random House Children's Books, a division of Penguin Random House LLC, 1745 Broadway, New York, NY 10019, and in Canada by Penguin Random House Canada Limited, Toronto. Golden Books, A Golden Book, and the G colophon are registered trademarks of Penguin Random House LLC.

ISBN 978-0-399-55892-4

randomhousekids.com

MANUFACTURED IN CHINA

10 9 8 7 6 5 4 3 2 1

Meet Poppy's Friends!

Troll Village is a colorful paradise where love is in the *hair* and Hug Time is celebrated every hour, on the hour! Poppy lives in Troll Village with all her friends. Use your stickers to complete this page and meet the Trolls!

POPPY

BIGGIE is a big Troll with a giant heart. He loves to dress up his pet, Mr. Dinkles, in adorable little outfits for photo shoots!

COOPER has a full coat of Troll hair that makes him especially magical! He also has wicked harmonica skills and crazy dance moves!

GUY DIAMOND is a living disco ball! He is covered in glitter and leaves a glitter trail wherever he goes!

SATIN AND CHENILLE

are fashion-forward twins connected by their brightly colored hair! Satin is pink and Chenille is blue.

BRANCH is very cautious. He has a highly camouflaged, heavily fortified Bergen-proof survival bunker!

DJ SUKI lays down the beats to create a totally unique sound. This mash-up expert has a cool jeweled belly button!

FUZZBERT is a Troll made entirely of hair (except for his cute little feet). He can use his whole body to tickle other Trolls!

SMIDGE is the smallest Troll with the mightiest hair and voice! She likes to lift weights and jump rope with her hair.

WHY SAY IT
WHEN YOU CAN SING IT?

Poppy is Troll Village's fearless and *pop*-timistic leader. She loves her friends!

Use the space below to draw
your own picture of Poppy!

FRIENDLY COMPETITION

WHO WILL WIN THE RACE?

Complete the maze on this page, and have a friend complete the maze on the opposite page. Time each other—or go at the same time!

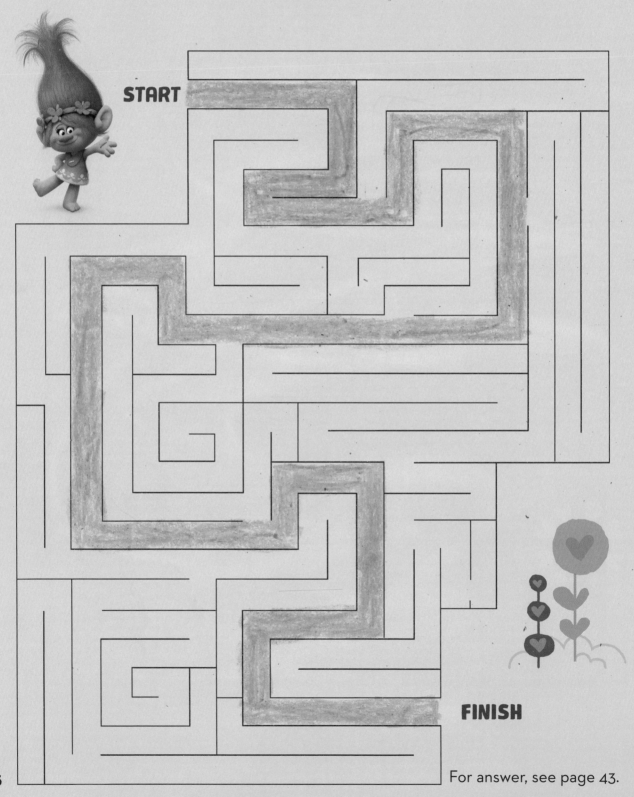

START

FINISH

6

For answer, see page 43.

FRIENDLY COMPETITION

WHO WILL WIN THE RACE?

Complete the maze on this page, and have a friend complete the maze on the opposite page. Time each other—or go at the same time!

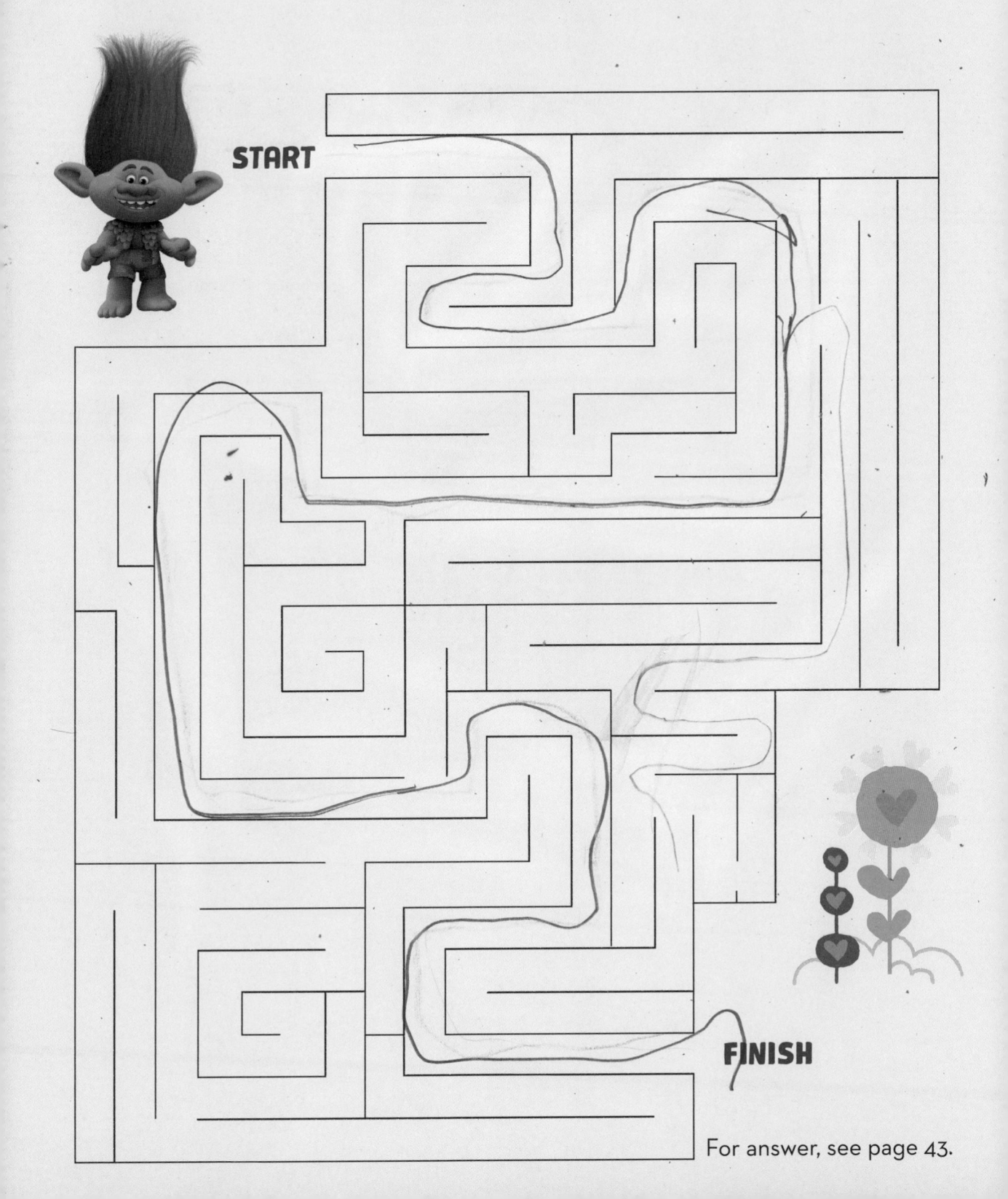

START

FINISH

For answer, see page 43.

TWO HEADS ARE BETTER THAN ONE!

Work with a friend to see who can come up with more words!

How many words can you make out of the letters in

CELEBRATION?

RAT

LIT

LET

BAT

BENT

BET

BIT

BITE

BRAIN

CAT

COT

CRAB

CRATE

LATE

LENT

LINT

NET

NOT

NOTE

RANT

RATE

For possible answers, see page 43.

What kind of Troll would you be?
Draw yourself as a Troll!

Look to Harper for guidance—
she's the village's resident artist!

Help Poppy deliver her Hug Day Friendship Cards by
unscrambling the name or names on each envelope.
Then draw a line from each invitation to the correct Troll!

 SATIN AND
NISTA DAN
LINECHLE
CHENILLE

BIGGIE AND MR. DINKLES

BIGGIE AND
GEBIGI DNA
RM. SKLINED
MR. DINKLES

SATIN AND CHENILLE

Branch
CRABNH

GUY DIAMOND

DJ SUKI
JD KISU

SMIDGE

GUY
UGY
NODDIAM
DIAMOND

BRANCH

Smidge
GIMEDS

DJ SUKI

12

For answer, see page 43.

ROCKIN' DAY

What do you like to do with your best pals? Use this space to plan the perfect day with the perfect sound track!

Activities

_____
_____
_____
_____
_____
_____

Set List

_____
_____
_____
_____
_____
_____

You're invited to this party!

13

Harper uses her hair like a giant paintbrush—so naturally, she's always covered in paint.

The Troll Village Art Studio seems to be missing some color. Help Harper fix that!

Draw something spectacular for Poppy as a Hug Day gift!

Unscramble the characters' names.
Then look across, down, and diagonally
to find them in the puzzle.

Y P O P P
P O P P Y ✓

C H R A N B
B R A N C H ✓

G E B G I I
B I G G I E ✓

P O C O R E
C O O P E R ✓

M R A A K
K A R M A ✓

S A I N T
S A T I N ✓

N I C H L E E L
C H E N I L L E ✓

G R I T D E B
B R I D G E T ✓

B R E Z F T U Z
F U Z Z B E R T ✓

M E G I D S
S M I D G E ✓

J D I S U K
D J S U K I ✓

P H E A R R
H A R P E R ✓

D Y M A D
M A D D Y ✓

Y U G M A D I N O D
G U Y D I A M O N D ✓

G I N K Y P P P E
K I N G P E P P Y ✓

I N G K S T R E I L G
K I N G G R I S T L E ✓

```
P P E A C Y B C G G W Q K
R O A F Z Z O C R R S U I
D J S U K I B E Y O P I N
S B A Z E H L I M B N E G
S R T Z O K I J G N I K P
M I I B R A N C H G O L E
I D N E L R N O H L I K P
D G Q R V M M O D E G E P
G E F T H A R P E R B M Y
E T K O C I P E O R A A B
Q U O O U W E R A P P D C
C H E N I L L E C B P D P
G U Y D I A M O N D X Y X
R K I N G G R I S T L E W
```

For answer, see page 43.

HUGFEST!

BERGEN BOXES OF LOVE

With a friend, take turns connecting two hearts with a straight line. If the line you draw completes a box, put your initials in it and take another turn. Count one point for squares containing your initials. If a box you completed contains a Troll, give yourself two points. When all the dots have been connected, the player with more points wins!

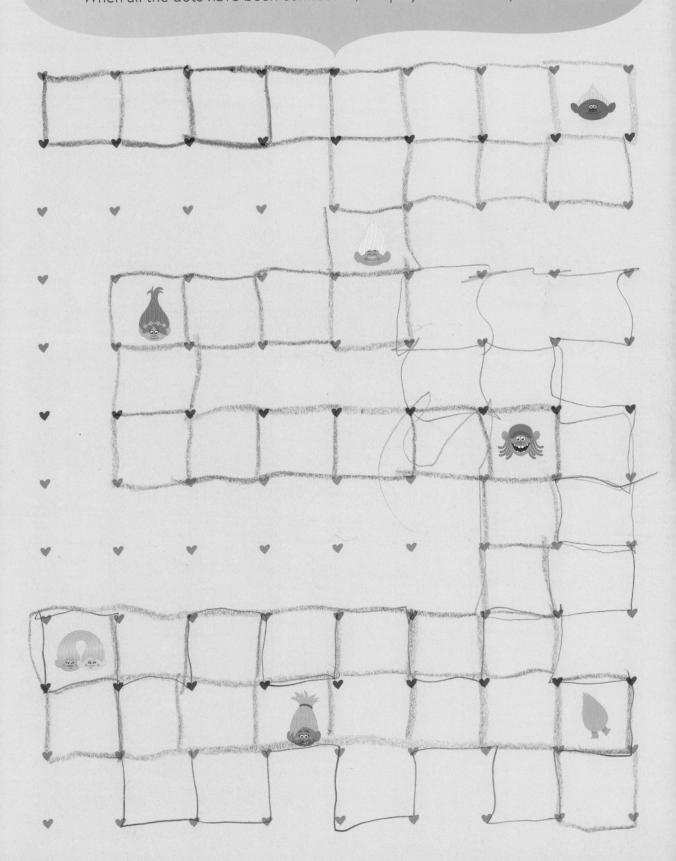

FRIENDLY COMPETITION

WHO CAN FIND MR. DINKLES FIRST?

Complete the maze on this page, and have a friend complete the maze on the opposite page. Time each other—or go at the same time!

START

FINISH

For answer, see page 43.

FRIENDLY COMPETITION

WHO CAN FIND MR. DINKLES FIRST?

Complete the maze on this page, and have a friend complete the maze on the opposite page. Time each other—or go at the same time!

WELCOME!

Welcome to Branch's bunker! Look at the two pictures.
Then circle the seven differences in the bottom one.

22

For answer, see page 43.

Branch's bunker is chock-full of resources, so the party doesn't stop! Look at both pictures. Then circle the seven differences in the bottom one.

For answer, see page 44.

Satin and Chenille
may have four hands
between them, but they
could use some help with
Poppy's wardrobe!

With a friend,
design your own
fabulous dresses
for Poppy
to wear.

A Bergen in Løve

To learn the name of King Gristle's love, follow the lines and write each letter in the correct box.

B R I D G E I

D E R B T I G

For answer, see page 44.

What are Poppy and her friends' two favorite things?

Start with the letter C. Going clockwise around the circle, write every third letter in order in the boxes.

CSEUWVPFDCRLAJHKOTEFBSHNARKYNTYDGPSYDILMNBRGVCIDFNRAGLP

C U P C A K E S   A N D
S I N G I N G

For answer, see page 44. **27**

Color this scene with a friend. Then use your stickers to complete it!

HARPER HAS ADVICE FOR ALL HER TROLL FRIENDS!

To complete the sentence, start with the letter T and, going counterclockwise around the circle, write every other letter in order in the boxes.

LET YOUR T R U E

C O L O R S   S H I N E !

30

For answer, see page 44.

Biggie and Mr. Dinkles

Friends Forever

TROLL TALK

What are Poppy, Guy Diamond, and Cooper talking about? Add words to the speech bubbles.

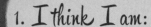

WHICH TROLL ARE YOU MOST LIKE?

Take this quiz to find out!

1. I think I am:
- A) an awesome advisor.
- B) someone with fashionable hair.
- C) totally groovy.
- D) artsy.
- E) outdoorsy.

2. My favorite thing to do is:
- A) state the obvious.
- B) get dressed up.
- C) dance, dance, dance!
- D) bring out the true colors in everything I see.
- E) explore nature.

3. My favorite outfit is:
- A) loose shirts and yoga pants.
- B) all of them!
- C) anything really colorful.
- D) something I made myself.
- E) animal-friendly.

4. My friends say I'm:
- A) full of wisdom.
- B) outgoing.
- C) a little weird.
- D) creative.
- E) totally organic!

5. If I went to Troll Village, I would:
- A) meditate on everything groovy.
- B) get a Troll party started . . . immediately!
- C) make friends and find out where the party is.
- D) pull out my sketchbook and start drawing.
- E) explore the natural wonders and befriend all creatures!

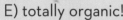

For answer, see page 44.

Cloud Friends

Poppy and Branch need Cloud Guy's help to choose the root tunnel that will take them to Bergen Town. Find the path that will get them closer to meeting their Bergen friends!

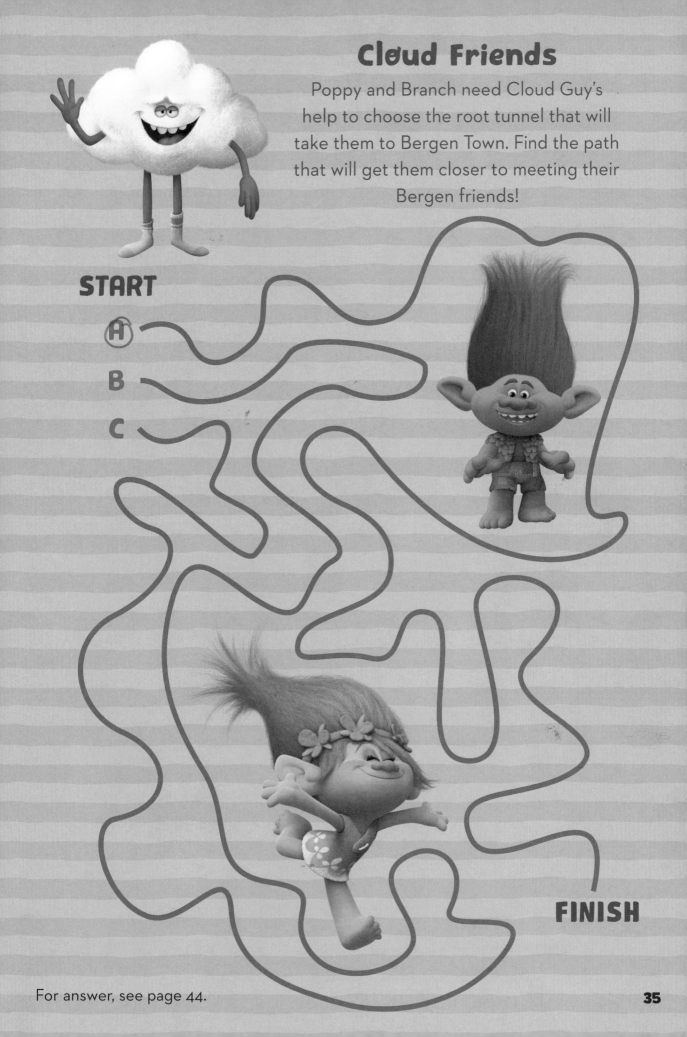

START

A
B
C

FINISH

For answer, see page 44.

BERGEN BOXES OF LOVE: ROUND 2

With a friend, take turns connecting two hearts with a straight line. If the line you draw completes a box, put your initials in it and take another turn. Count one point for squares containing your initials. If a box you completed contains a Troll, give yourself two points. When all the dots have been connected, the player with more points wins!

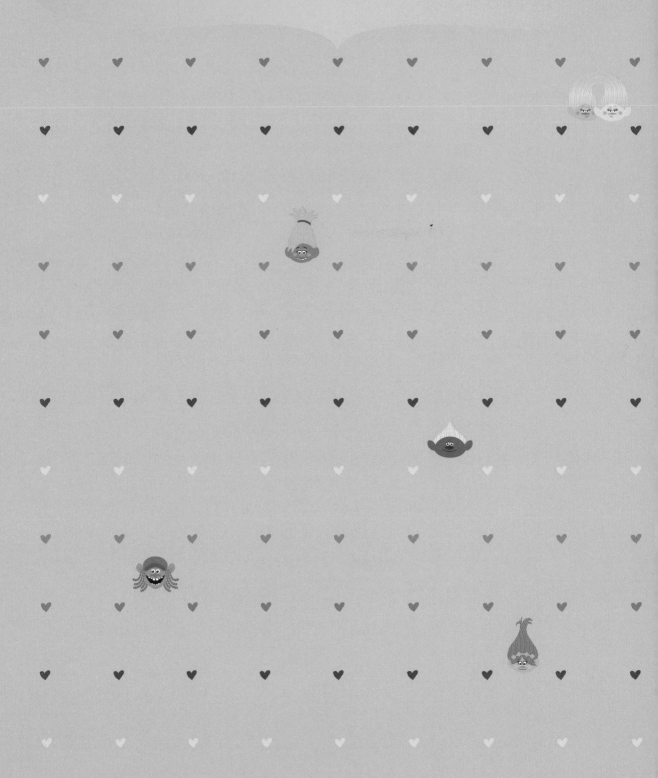

Searching High and Low for Friends

Look up, down,
forward, and backward to find all the Trolls!

POPPY · BRANCH · COOPER · FUZZBERT · HARPER · BIGGIE
MR. DINKLES · SATIN AND CHENILLE · SMIDGE · GUY DIAMOND
MADDY · CYBIL · KARMA · DJ SUKI

```
T P H G E E K L D C M I L L U V Q U O O D A X Y F F
E M E S W I A P P O P P Y A H C N B I L M A G H R E
G P K J N D Z P O O M B R L C J M A L W R I D B A H
D R L U W C S R L P R T L N E E S S P B D D N C D C
I K S E V M I E C E V E T R E B Z Z U F I M O N W E
R I V V H A R P E R D H F I I M W L P O N F M S E N
B N S Y P O K E E W C K E R G G E D D O K I A C K L
A G S S R O K W Q I Y C E D G D D L J K L Z I Z Z D
C G Z Y X Q U G H I B M N P I O D X S L E G D I M S
F R A Z W N R T B L I I M O B V U T U T S Y Y Q N I
B I K G E M J W F I L L P M E W H U K T F D U S T R
M S A T I N A N D C H E N I L L E M I S L D G E U I
C T J R S F G M W K A R M A E I H G N A N A A O T T
J L C H C N A R B T H I H N K G A L O P W M M E A H
S E A M I N M P B K D W H E T K B L A U I P M F I G
```

Bonus points if you can find
the Bergens in the puzzle!

BRIDGET · KING GRISTLE

For answer, see page 44.

WORD QUEST FOR LOVE

Find a path through the word grid using the words and phrases listed below. Go up, down, forward, and backward (but not diagonally). Use the final letter in each word or phrase to start the next one listed. Rearrange the eleven letters left over to learn the name of Bridget's true love!

HUG TIME • ENERGETIC • CUPCAKES AND RAINBOWS • SINGING
GLITTER • RAINBOW SPOOL • LOVE • EXCITED • DARING
GREAT MUSIC • COLORFUL FLOWERS • SCRAPBOOKING

START

H	U	N	I	N	L	T	E	R
T	G	G	S	G	I	T	I	A
I	M	E	W	I	L	I	N	B
E	G	N	O	N	G	S	W	O
T	R	E	B	N	I	P	L	O
I	A	N	D	R	A	O	O	V
C	S	K	E	T	I	C	X	E
U	E	A	D	S	A	T	M	U
P	R	R	I	R	E	R	I	S
C	A	I	N	G	U	F	C	O
E	W	O	L	F	L	R	O	L
R	T	A	P	B	G	I	N	G
S	C	R	E	O	K			**FINISH**

king gristle

38   For answer, see page 44.

HAIR FOR EACH OTHER!

BFF CODE

Use the key to decipher the code and reveal the clues. Then use the clues to solve the riddle!

This **R O Y A L** Troll likes

to say, "**W H Y   S A Y** it

W H E N   Y O U   C A N

S I N G it?"

_P O P P Y_

Who is this riddle about?

For answer, see page 44.

BOXES WITH FRIENDS

Use your stickers to finish the puzzle. Fill in the grid so that Poppy, Guy Diamond, Branch, and DJ Suki appear only once in each row, column, and box of four squares.

Guy Diamond

DJ Suki

Branch

Branch

DJ Suki

Guy Diamond

Poppy

For answer, see page 44.

ANSWERS

Pages 6 and 7

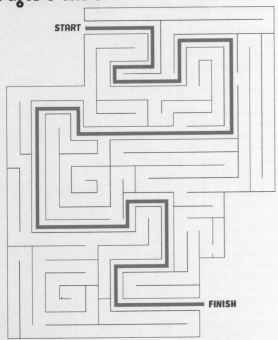

START

FINISH

Pages 6 (continued) — Page 16 (continued)

Page 16 (continued)

Page 8

Possible answers: Bat, bent, bet, bit, bite, brain, cat, cot, crab, crate, late, lent, let, lint, lit, net, not, note, rant, rat, rate, react, rent, rot, and train.

Page 12

NISTA DAN LINECHLE: Satin and Chenille

GEBIGI DNA RM. SKLINED: Biggie and Mr. Dinkles

CRABNH: Branch

JD KISU: DJ Suki

UGY NODDIAM: Guy Diamond

GIMEDS: Smidge

Pages 20 and 21

START

FINISH

Page 16

YPOPP
POPPY

CHRANB
BRANCH

GEBGII
BIGGIE

POCORE
COOPER

MRAAK
KARMA

SAINT
SATIN

NICHLEEL
CHENILLE

GRITDEB
BRIDGET

BREZFTUZ
FUZZBERT

MEGIDS
SMIDGE

JD ISUK
DJ SUKI

PHEARR
HARPER

DYMAD
MADDY

YUG MADINOD
GUY DIAMOND

GINK YPPPE
KING PEPPY

INGK STREILG
KING GRISTLE

Page 22

Page 23

Page 26
Bridget.

Page 27
Cupcakes and singing.

Page 30
Let your true colors shine!

Page 34
If you answered with:
Mostly As: You're like Cybil!
Mostly Bs: You're like Poppy!
Mostly Cs: You're like Cooper!
Mostly Ds: You're like Harper!
Mostly Es: You're like Karma!

Page 35
A.

Page 37

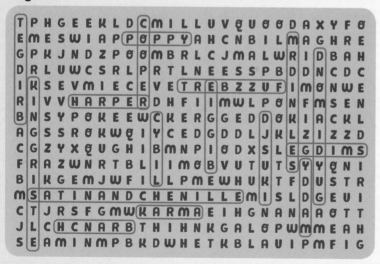

Page 38 King Gristle.

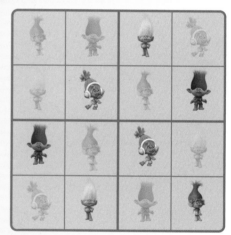

Page 41
This royal Troll likes to say, "Why say it when you can sing it?";
Poppy.

Page 42

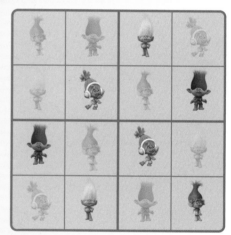

Poppy would never leave
any of her friends out!
Here are some extra cards
if you need them.

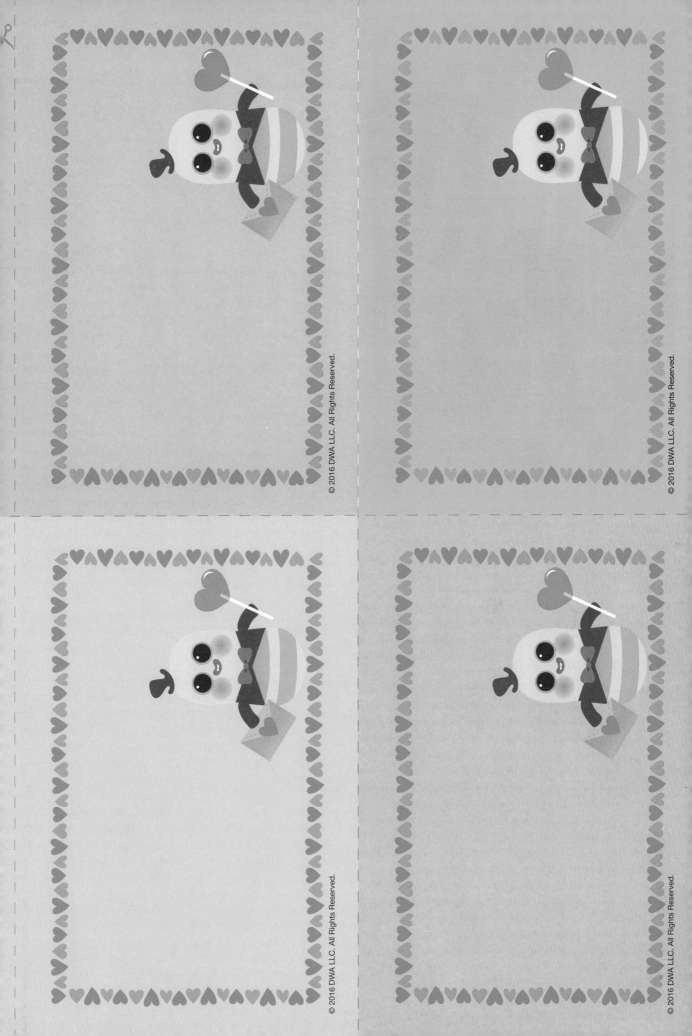